OLIVER, THE SPACESHIP, AND ME

LYNN ROWE REED

Holiday House / New York

To Steve and Kathy Rowe

Text and illustrations copyright © 2009 by Lynn Rowe Reed
All Rights Reserved
Printed and Bound in China
The text typeface is Billy Regular.
The illustrations were painted in acrylic on canvas and digitally reproduced.
The remaining elements were scanned and/or photographed and incorporated
in Photoshop. Some of the items incorporated include steel pieces,
wire, pvc pipe, welding gloves, tin snips, coins, and glass tiles.
The spaceship blueprint was created by the architectural firm
Grinsfelder Associates Inc., of Fort Wayne, Indiana.
www.holidayhouse.com
First Edition
1 3 5 7 9 10 8 6 4 2

Library of Congress Cataloging-in-Publication Data
Reed, Lynn Rowe.
Oliver, the spaceship, and me / written and illustrated by Lynn Rowe Reed. — 1st ed.
p. cm.
Summary: A boy builds a spaceship and promises the first ride to everyone
who helps him, but when blastoff time comes, he decides to take his best friend instead.
ISBN 978-0-8234-2193-0 (hardcover)
[1. Spaceships—Fiction. 2. Best friends—Fiction. 3. Friendship—Fiction.] I. Title.
PZ7.R252730I 2009
[E]—dc22
2008022614

My best friend, Oliver,
lives next door.
Oliver and I love all
of the same things—
especially planning to be
astronauts someday.

For his birthday,
Oliver gets to choose
one friend to take to
the planetarium.

Of course
he picks . . .

Kevin Shipman!

DRAT!

I am bopping mad and flapping furious.

I am going to get even!

I am going to build a spaceship—
an actual flying spaceship—

and go
into space . . .

without
Oliver.

I begin by drawing my spaceship.

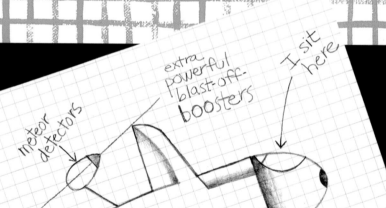

The next morning, I make a list.

MY TO DO LIST :
(for building a spaceship)
1. get a blueprint   engineer
2. cut metal parts   metal worker
3. weld parts together   welder
4. plumbing   plumber
5. electricity   electrician

P.S. Maybe I'll think of
    more later.

To Space without Oliver

OLIVER STINKS!

I schedule an appointment with my Uncle Drew, an engineer. He takes my drawing and puts the information into his computer.

Then he prints a fancy blueprint that shows every detail and measurement for my spaceship. I offer to pay him, but he says, "No thanks, Carter, just give me the first ride."

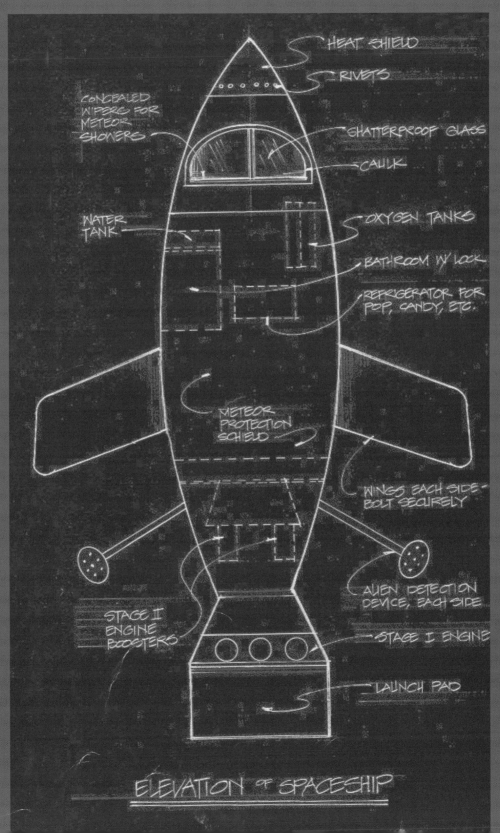

① get a blueprint   engineer

② cut metal parts   metal worker

Next, I'm off to the sheet
metal worker's shop.
I show my blueprint
to Mr. Cutler.

FLAMMABLE

He cuts pieces of steel from large sheets and helps me load them into a cart.

I wheel the cart back and forth to a welding shop, where I leave the pieces each time.

When I leave Mr. Cutler's for the last time, I say, "Thanks! What do I owe you?" He says, "How about the first ride?"

The next morning, I'm off to the welder's shop. Ms. Joiner and I wear helmets while she uses a fancy gun to squirt hot, fluid metal to join the pieces.

When she is finished, my spaceship is so big that she has to load it onto a flatbed truck. She drives it to my house.

We hide it behind
the garage.
"I'll give you the first
ride," I tell Ms. Joiner.
"See you at
blastoff, Carter,"
she says.

Next, I call the plumber, Mr. Waters. He brings lots of pipe, a water storage tank, and a big pump.

① get a blueprint
② cut metal parts
③ weld parts together
④ plumbing

He cuts pipe, bends it, twists it, joins it, and—voilà!— my spaceship has water and . . .

a bathroom with a shower.

"I'll come along on the first ride," Mr. Waters hollers, driving away. "See you at the countdown!"

My next trip is to the electrician. I bring pictures of my spaceship to convince Mr. Sparks to help. "I suppose since you've gotten *this* far . . . ," Mr. Sparks says, and takes me home in his truck full of electrical supplies. He installs a circuit breaker and runs wire throughout the spaceship.

He has lots of special gear to protect us from the electricity while he works.

VOLTAGE

Before long, Mr. Sparks is finished and says, "I'll ride along on your first trip!"

I am now the commander of an actual flying spaceship, but there's still something missing. I call my Aunt Tracey, who is an amazing artist. She brings paint chips, carpet samples, and designs to choose from. A few decisions are made, and Aunt Tracey turns my spaceship into a masterpiece.

The night before blastoff, I toss and turn. In the morning, I put on my space suit.

There is noise coming from my backyard.

A crowd has gathered. My parents wonder what is going on, but they are too speechless to ask. I, however, make a speech about dreams, about working toward goals . . . and about friendship.

I had a dream about FLYING...blah blah blah...I worked hard... blah blah...not possible without friends...blah blah....

I open the door to my spaceship and, suddenly,

I realize my one and only design flaw: The spaceship only has *two* seats!

OOPS.

"I can only take one of you with me."
I apologize. I ponder: Who had helped the
most—engineer, metal worker, welder, plumber,
electrician, or artist? My head spins
and my innards twist.

I make my choice.

As we climb into our seats for blastoff, I throw my arm around Oliver and say, "Fasten your seat belt, buddy. It could get a little bumpy!" And then we . . .

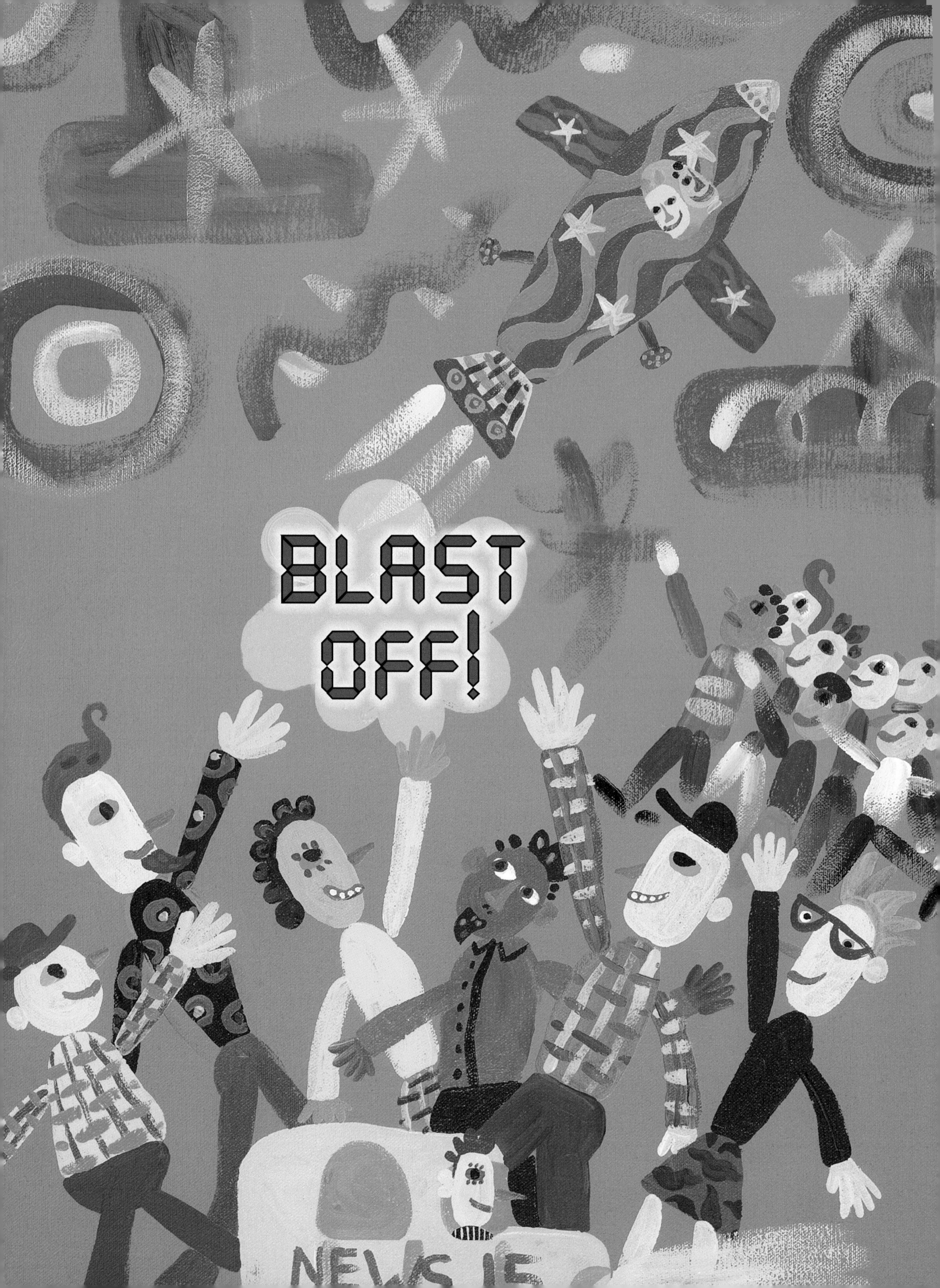
BLAST
OFF!